THIS EDITION PUBLISHED BY PARRAGON BOOKS LTD IN 2014
AND DISTRIBUTED BY

PARRAGON INC.
440 PARK AVENUE SOUTH, 13TH FLOOR
NEW YORK, NY 10016
WWW.PARRAGON.COM

EDITED BY MICHAEL DIGGLE
DESIGNED BY ALEX DIMOND
PRODUCTION BY RICHARD WHEELER

ISBN 978-1-4723-6469-2

PRINTED IN CHINA

T-REX TERROR

THE SUPERSAURUS LEGEND BEGINS ...

WRITTEN BY
TIMOTHY KNAPMAN

ILLUSTRATED BY
TIM WESSON

PaRragon

Bath · New York · Cologne · Melbourne · Delhi
Hong Kong · Shenzhen · Singapore · Amsterdam

65 million years ago …

A radioactive meteorite hurtles through outer space, heading straight for planet Earth …

And the bustling dinotropolis of New Dino City!

IS IT A PTERODACTYL?

IS IT A PLANE?

ARE WE GOING TO BECOME EXTINCT?

Meanwhile, in Cretaceous Park, four young dinos are playing dinoball, but their lives are about to CHANGE FOREVER!

Too late! Before they can escape, the meteorite hits with a deafening ...

KA-BOOM!

... zapping the young dinos with its galactic superpowers!

The four friends walk home, full of questions ...

Suddenly, from a nearby bank, they hear a cry for ...

It's another Raptor robbery! But if those pesky predators think they'll get away THIS time, they're in for a SUPER surprise ...

And in that electrifying moment, the LEGEND begins!

In no time, the SUPERSAURS are the talk of New Dino City ...

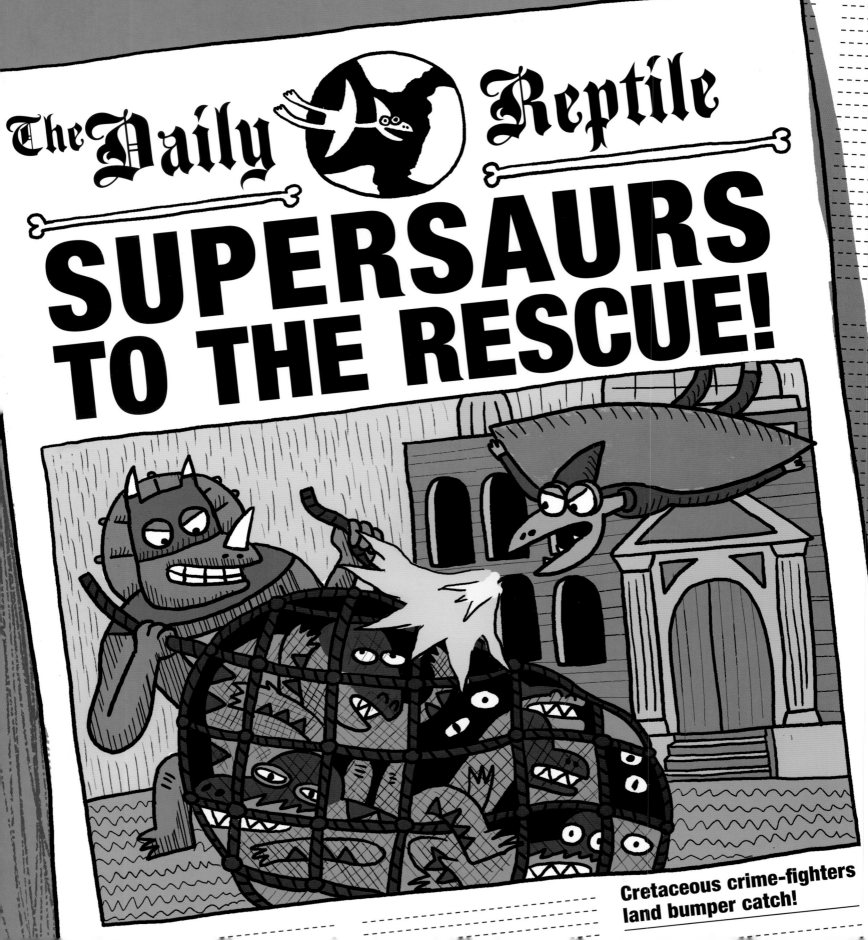

Before long, the Supersaurs have rid New Dino City of crime, and things are all quiet at Supersaurus HQ.

Doc loves his gadgets, but there's something not quite right about this giveaway ...

Back at Supersaurus HQ, Trix is monitoring the bay around New Dino City. He's picked up some movement on Volcano Island.

When suddenly, every monitor is tuned to …

The Supersaurs spring into action!

With only seconds to spare, Terra's fireball smashes the rocket out of the sky!

And so the city is safe ... until next time!